This **Frog** book belongs to:

....

Translated by Anthea Bell

This paperback edition first published in 2014 by Andersen Press Ltd.
First published in Great Britain in 1989 by Andersen Press Ltd.,
20 Vauxhall Bridge Road, London SW1V 2SA.
Published in Australia by Random House Australia Pty.,
Level 3, 100 Pacific Highway, North Sydney, NSW 2060.
Copyright © Max Velthuijs Foundation, 1989

Colour separated in Switzerland by Photolitho AG, Zürich.
Printed and bound in China by Foshan Zhao Rong printing Co., Ltd.

10   9   8   7   6   5   4   3   2   1

British Library Cataloguing in Publication Data available.
ISBN 978 1 78344 145 7

Frog
in Love

Max Velthuijs

Andersen Press

Frog was sitting on the river bank.
He felt funny. He didn't know if he was happy
or sad.

He had been walking about in a dream all week.
What could be wrong with him?

Then he met Pig.

"Hello, Frog," said Pig. "You don't look very well.
What's the matter with you?"

"I don't know," said Frog. "I feel like laughing and
crying at the same time. And there's something
going thump-thump inside me, here."

"Maybe you've caught a cold," said Pig.
"You'd better go home to bed."
Frog went on his way. He was worried.

Then he passed Hare's house.

"Hare," he said, "I don't feel well."

"Come along in and sit down," said Hare, kindly.

"Now then," said Hare, "what's the matter with you?"

"Sometimes I go hot, and sometimes I go cold,"
said Frog, "and there's something going thump-thump
inside me, here." And he put his hand on his chest.

Hare thought hard, just like a real doctor.

"I see," he said. "It's your heart. Mine goes thump-thump too."

"But mine sometimes thumps faster than usual," said Frog.

"It goes one-two, one-two, one-two."

Hare took a big book down from his bookshelf and
turned the pages. "Aha!" he said. "Listen to this. Heartbeat,
speeded up, hot and cold turns . . . it means you're in love!"

"In love?" said Frog, surprised. "Wow! I'm in love!"

And he was so pleased that he did a tremendous jump,

right out of the door and up in the air.

Pig was quite scared when Frog suddenly came falling
from the sky.
"You seem to be better," said Pig.
"I am! I feel just fine," said Frog. "I'm in love!"
"Well, that's good news. Who are you in love with?"
asked Pig. Frog hadn't stopped to think about that.

"I know!" he said. "I'm in love with the pretty,
nice, lovely white duck!"
"You can't be," said Pig. "A frog can't be in love
with a duck. You're green and she's white."
But Frog didn't let that bother him.

He couldn't write, but he could do beautiful paintings. Back at home he painted a lovely picture, with red and blue in it and lots of green, his favourite colour.

In the evening, when it was dark, he went out
with his picture and pushed it under the door
of Duck's house.
His heart was beating hard with excitement.

Duck was very surprised when she found the picture.
"Who can have sent me this beautiful picture?"
she cried, and she hung it on the wall.

Next day Frog picked a beautiful bunch of flowers.
He was going to give them to Duck.
But when he reached her door, he felt too shy to face
her. He put the flowers down on the doorstep and ran
away as fast as he could go.
And so it went on, day after day.
Frog just couldn't pluck up the courage to speak.

Duck was very pleased with all her lovely presents.
But who could be sending them?

Poor Frog!
He didn't enjoy his food any more, and he couldn't sleep at night.
Things went on like this for weeks.

How could he show Duck he loved her?
"I must do something nobody else can do," he decided.
"I must break the world high jump record! Dear Duck
will be very surprised, and then she'll love me back."

Frog started training at once.
He practised the high jump for days on end.
He jumped higher and higher, right up to the clouds.
No frog in the world had ever jumped so high before.

"What can be the matter with Frog?" asked Duck, worried. "Jumping like that is dangerous. He'll do himself an injury."
She was right.

At thirteen minutes past two on Friday afternoon, things went wrong. Frog was doing the highest jump in history when he lost his balance and fell to the ground.
Duck, who happened to be passing at the time, came hurrying up to help him.

Frog could hardly walk. Supporting him carefully, she took him home with her. She nursed him with tender loving care.

"Oh, Frog, you might have been killed!" she said. "You really must be careful. I'm so fond of you!"

And then, at last, Frog plucked up his courage.

"I'm very fond of you too, dear Duck," he stammered. His heart was going thump-thump faster than ever, and his face turned deep green.

Ever since then, they have loved each other dearly.
A frog and a duck . . .
Green and white.
Love knows no boundaries.

Max Velthuijs's twelve beautiful stories about **Frog** and his friends first started to appear twenty five years ago and are now available as paperbacks, e-books and apps.

9781783441440
9781783441532
9781783441501
9781783441426
9781783441471
9781783441457
9781783441525
97811783441433
9781783441518
9781783441495
9781783441488
9781783441419

Max Velthuijs (Dutch for Field House) lived in the Netherlands, and received the prestigious Hans Christian Andersen Medal for Illustration. His charming stories capture childhood experiences while offering life lessons to children as young as three, and have been translated into more than forty languages.

'Frog is an inspired creation – a masterpiece of graphic simplicity.' GUARDIAN

'Miniature morality plays for our age.' IBBY